HAPPY BIRTHDAY

David Martin ILLUSTRATED BY Scott Nash

Introduction

Before your child starts reading, read this story
description. Then look through the book together
and talk about the pictures.

This story is called *Happy Birthday.*
It's about all the birthday presents
Monkey makes for Mom, including a
special picture. What does it say?

Monkey makes a cake for Mom.

"Happy Birthday, Mom."

Monkey makes a birdhouse for Mom.

"Happy Birthday, Mom."

Monkey makes a hat for Mom.

"Happy Birthday, Mom."

Monkey paints a picture for Mom.

"I love you, Monkey," says Mom.